First published in the United States of America in 2014 by Chronicle Books LLC.
Originally published in France in 2011 by Rue du monde under the title *Au même instant, sur la Terre . . .*

Text and illustrations on pages 5–31, plus illustration on front of map, copyright © 2011 by Rue du monde.
Illustrations on cover, endpapers, pages 32–33, and map, plus the pattern on pages 4–5, copyright © 2014 by Clotilde Perrin.
Translation, and text on pages 32–33, copyright © 2014 by Chronicle Books LLC.

Library-of-Congress Cataloging-in-Publication Data available.
ISBN 978-1-4521-2208-3

Manufactured in China.

FSC
www.fsc.org

MIX
Paper from responsible sources
FSC® C008047

Design by Ryan Hayes.
Typeset in Mr. Eaves.
The illustrations in this book were rendered in pencil and colorized digitally.

10  9  8  7  6

Chronicle Books LLC
680 Second Street
San Francisco, CA 94107

Chronicle Books—we see things differently. Become part of our community at www.chroniclekids.com.

# AT THE SAME MOMENT, AROUND THE WORLD

by Clotilde Perrin

chronicle books · san francisco

It is six o'clock in the morning in Dakar, Senegal. Keita wakes up early to help his father count the fish caught during the night.

At the same moment, in Paris, France, it is seven o'clock in the morning, and Benedict drinks hot chocolate before school.

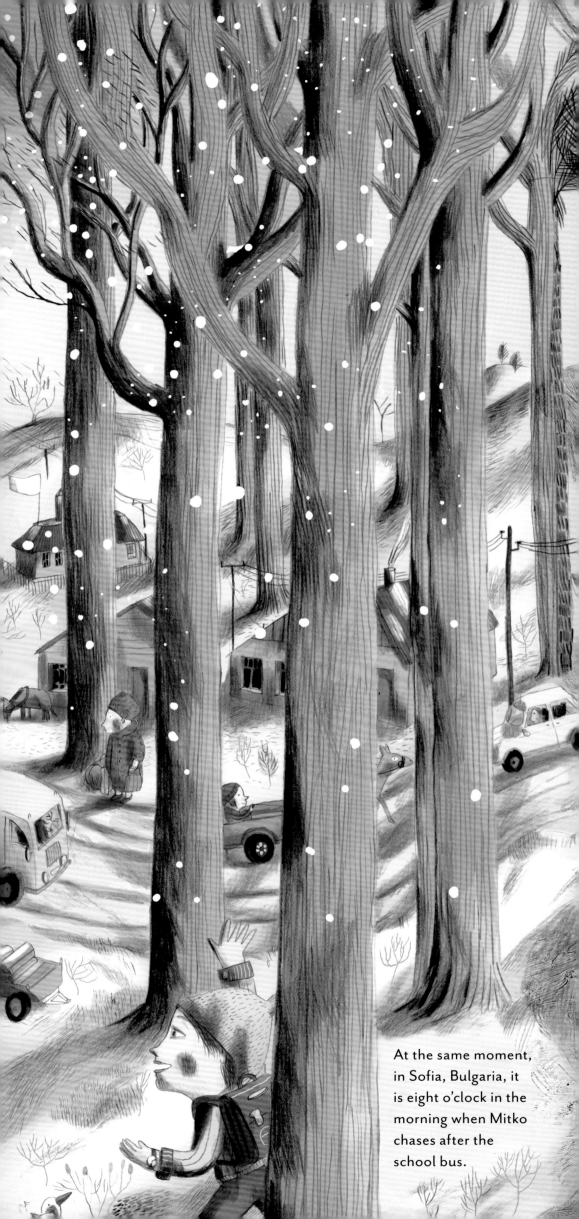

At the same moment, in Sofia, Bulgaria, it is eight o'clock in the morning when Mitko chases after the school bus.

At the same moment, in Baghdad, Iraq, it is nine o'clock in the morning, and Yasmine plays while her mother shops at the market.

At the same moment, in Dubai, United Arab Emirates, it is ten o'clock in the morning, and Nadia watches workers construct a new building.

At the same moment,
in Samarkand, Uzbekistan,
it is eleven o'clock in the
morning, and Ravshan and
Yuliya return from their visit
to a nearby market.

At the same moment, in the Himalayan Mountains near the towering Mount Everest, it is noon, and Lilu eats lunch with her mother.

At the same moment,
in Hanoi, Vietnam, it is
one o'clock in the afternoon,
and Khanh takes a nap despite
noise on the street outside.

At the same moment,
in Shanghai, China,
it is two o'clock in the
afternoon, and Chen
practices for the Lunar
New Year parade.

At the same moment, near Tokyo, Japan, it is three o'clock in the afternoon, and Keiko admires the *koinobori*, or carp streamers, blowing in the wind.

At the same moment, in the desert
between Ayers Rock and Sydney, Australia,
it is four o'clock in the afternoon, and
Kate drives toward the beach.

At the same moment, in Nouméa, New Caledonia, it is five o'clock in the evening, and Matea and Joany make music together.

At the same moment, in Anadyr, Russia, it is six o'clock in the evening when Ivan takes his dog for a walk around the neighborhood.

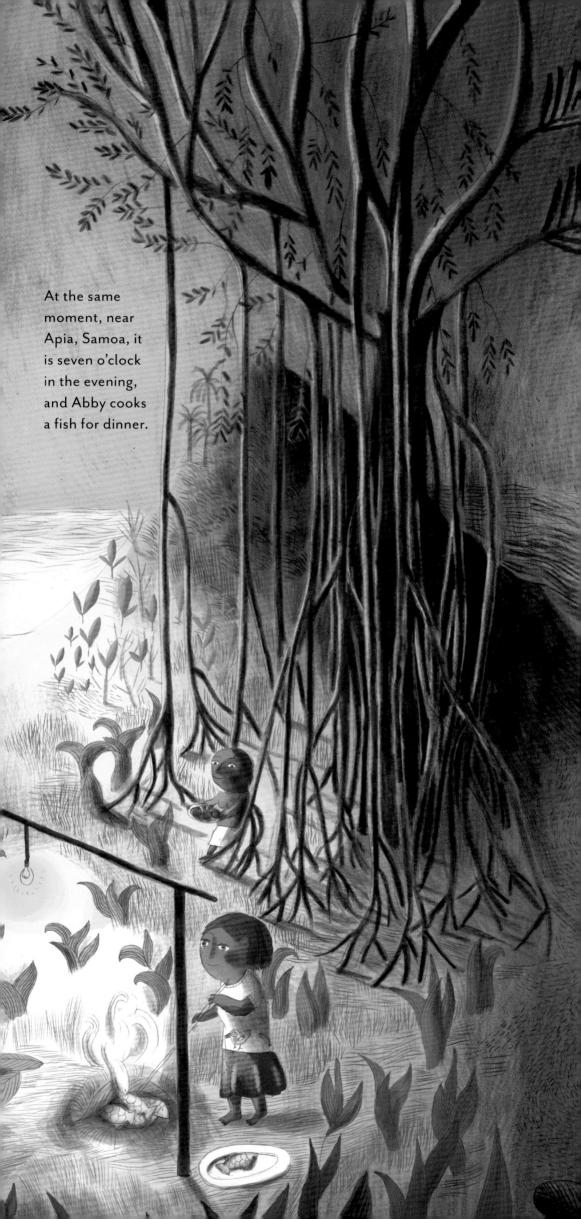

At the same moment, near Apia, Samoa, it is seven o'clock in the evening, and Abby cooks a fish for dinner.

At the same moment, in Honolulu, Hawaii, it is eight o'clock in the evening when Allen and Kiana enjoy the very last rays of sun.

At the same moment, in Anchorage, Alaska, it is nine o'clock in the evening when William blows on his bedtime tea.

At the same moment, in San Francisco, California, it is ten o'clock at night when Sharon and Peter kiss good bye.

At the same moment, in Phoenix, Arizona, it is eleven o'clock at night, and Samantha watches the desert pass by from the train.

At the same moment,
it is midnight in
Mexico City, Mexico,
and Pablo has
magical dreams.

At the same moment, in Lima, Peru,
it is one o'clock in the morning when
baby Diego is born!

At the same moment, in the Amazon rainforest near Manaus, Brazil, it is two o'clock in the morning when Ana has quite a shock!

At the same moment, in
Nuuk, Greenland, it is three o'clock
in the morning, and Lexi can't sleep.

At the same moment, on the island
of Fernando de Noronha near Brazil,
it is four o'clock in the morning, and
Antonio is sleeping soundly.

At the same moment, on a ship in the
middle of the Atlantic Ocean, it is five
o'clock in the morning when Chloé finds
herself tired from dancing all night.

# ABOUT TIME ZONES

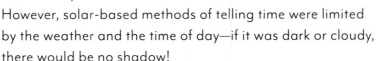

### Early Timekeeping

Long ago, people told time by the sun, moon, and stars. Telling time by where the sun was in the sky, called solar time, was most common. Eventually people developed sun clocks, or shadow clocks, to help them keep time by the sun. Ancient Egyptians erected obelisks, tall monuments to the sun god, Ra, that cast long shadows by which they could tell time. Sundials, another timekeeping invention, were often portable and even more accurate. However, solar-based methods of telling time were limited by the weather and the time of day—if it was dark or cloudy, there would be no shadow!

For this reason people developed other tools for telling time. They developed water clocks, which poured water at a certain rate, or used the length of time it took a candle or oil lamp to burn to track how much time had passed. The pendulum clock was invented in the 17th century, and soon other mechanical clocks were developed as well.

### The Invention of Time Zones

Because the sun rises and sets at different times in different places due to the rotation of the Earth, clocks set by the sun aren't accurate between regions. For example, when using solar time, the time in New York and Boston differs by about eight minutes. But imagine if you were traveling farther! The differences would be greater, making solar time even more inaccurate. Once communication by telegraph and travel by train became more common, the small differences in solar time between regions became problematic. Can you imagine not knowing when a train would arrive or depart?

Several different people came up with the idea of establishing time zones, but Sir Sandford Fleming is generally credited with the invention. He proposed a worldwide system of time zones based around a 24-hour clock using Greenwich, England, at 0 degrees longitude as the reference point. He presented his idea to the International Meridian Conference in 1884, at which time Greenwich was established as the prime meridian.

Each time zone is a vertical section of the globe from the North Pole to the South Pole. But the time zones aren't always a straight line—this is to make sure one city isn't separated in to two time zones! Most time zones are 15 degrees apart from one another (a sphere like the Earth has 360 degrees, which when divided by 24 time zones, equals 15 degrees per time zone!), but large countries like China and India, for example, choose to use one time zone for the whole country.

Each standard time zone is one hour apart from the next standard time zone. If you were heading east from the prime meridian, you would add an hour to whatever time it is in Greenwich, England, for each time zone you pass. If you were heading west from the prime meridian, you would subtract an hour from the time in Greenwich, England, for each time zone you pass. Some areas observe daylight saving time, which is when a time zone changes their clocks at certain times of the year to take advantage of the natural sunlight. When an area observes daylight saving time, the standard one-hour time difference between time zones can change.

## Accurate Timekeeping

We now use Coordinate Universal Time, or UTC, rather than Greenwich Mean Time, or GMT. UTC is measured by atomic clocks and uses leap seconds to account for gradual slowing in the Earth's rotation, so it is more accurate than GMT but still uses the prime meridian as its reference point. There are now about 40 time zones in the world (some of these time zones are not a full hour apart from one another, but 15, 30, or 45 minutes from a neighboring time zone).

Today we have the ability to measure and synchronize time more accurately than ever before. For example, quartz watches and clocks are accurate to better than one second, and atomic clocks are accurate to one trillionth of a second, per day. This level of accuracy allows for technology like the Global Positioning System, or GPS—technology powered by a satellite that can tell where you are at any given moment in time—to function.

LIFT FOR A

WORLD
MAP